DATE DUE			

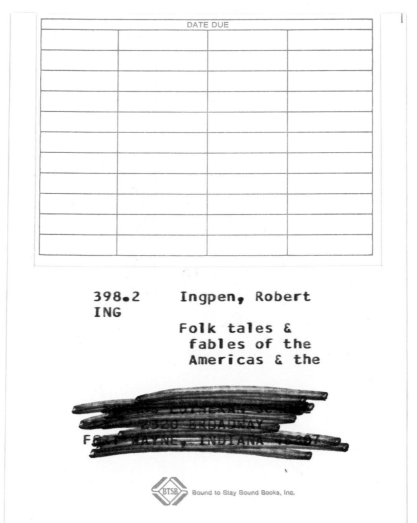

FOLK·TALES·&·FABLES·OF
THE AMERICAS
& THE PACIFIC

FOLK·TALES·&·FABLES·OF THE AMERICAS & THE PACIFIC

Robert Ingpen & Barbara Hayes

CHELSEA HOUSE PUBLISHERS
New York • Philadelphia

First published in the United States in 1994
by Chelsea House Publishers

© Copyright David Bateman Ltd & Dragon's World 1994

First Printing
1 3 5 7 9 8 6 4 2

Text Editor Molly Perham
Editor Diana Briscoe
Art Director Dave Allen
Editorial Director Pippa Rubinstein

ISBN 0-7910-2759-7

Typeset in Bookman.
Printed in Italy

Contents

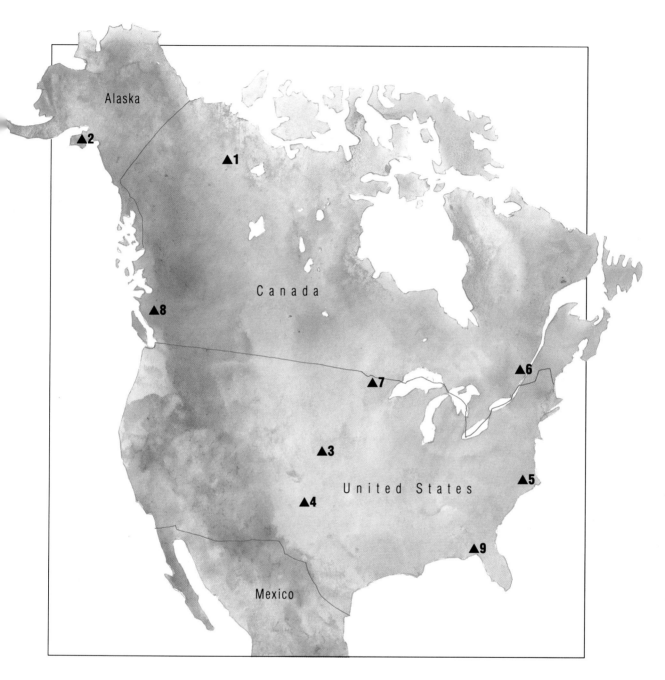

North America

1

The Crow and the Daylight

This is a story told by the Inuit, or Eskimo, of northern Canada. In those lands of ice and snow, for half of the year the sun does not rise above the horizon and darkness covers the land. For the remaining months the sun never sets and there is continuous daylight.

Many, many years ago, when the world began, there was no daylight in the lands of the far North. The Inuit lived in the dark, with only faint glimmers of light from their seal-oil lamps to see by. They did not know when they should get up, nor when they should go to bed, because there was no day and no night.

A very wise crow lived in one of the villages. He had learned to talk and was much respected by all the people. Sometimes the crow would tell stories of the wonders he had seen on journeys to other lands. That is how the Inuit first heard about daylight.

'What is daylight?' they asked.

'Where there is daylight people can see all around,' the crow replied. 'They can see the whole countryside. They can even see animals a long way off.'

The Inuit thought that daylight sounded like a very good thing. 'How much easier hunting would be!' they said. 'How much safer we would be if we could see the polar bears before they attack us! If only we had daylight here in our land.'

They gathered round the crow and begged him to fetch some daylight for them.

At first the crow refused. 'It is a long flight to the land of daylight,' he said. 'And even if I arrived safely, they might not give me any.'

The Inuit begged and pleaded and at last the crow agreed to go. After a rest and a meal, he flew up into the black sky and turned towards the east, where daylight comes from.

After travelling for many days, the crow saw a dim light above the horizon. He flew on still until the sky was all lit up and he could see the ground beneath him. Light shone from a large snowhouse belonging to a village chief.

By now the crow was exhausted, so he settled in a tree to rest. Just then a young woman left the large snowhouse and walked to the river to fetch water. As the crow watched, she dipped a seal-skin bucket through a hole in the ice to haul up some water.

The crow slipped from his perch. He shook off his skin and turned himself into a tiny speck of dust, dancing in a beam of light. As the chief's daughter walked back with her bucket of water, the speck of dust settled on her dress and was carried into the house.

Inside it was warm and flooded with light. The chief sat watching his best-loved grandson crawling around on a bearskin rug. The baby played with his toy animals and kayaks carved from walrus ivory, putting them all into an ivory box and laughing with delight as he tipped them out again.

When the young woman put down the bucket of water to pick up her son, the speck of dust drifted from her dress into the baby's ear. The baby began to cry.

The chief, who loved the child dearly, frowned and asked what was wrong.

'Ask to be given some daylight to play with,' whispered the speck of dust in the baby's ear.

The baby asked for daylight. The chief smiled and told his daughter to untie the rawhide string, that secured his leather hunting bag. Inside was a wooden box with pictures of all the brave things the chief had done carved on the sides.

The baby smiled at the pictures as his mother showed them to him. But then he started to cry and ask for daylight. The chief could refuse his best-loved grandson nothing, so he told his daughter to open the box and give the baby one of the shining balls that were kept inside.

Once more the speck of dust whispered in the baby's ear. 'Ask for some string to tie around the ball,' it said.

The baby asked for string. Now he played happily, dangling the bright ball on the string. The chief and his daughter stepped outside, leaving the door open so that the baby could call to them if it wished.

This was the opportunity that the crow had been hoping for.

'Play near the doorway,' the crow whispered to the baby.

The baby played near the door.

'Go and play outside. Take the daylight with you and swing it in the breeze.'

As the baby crawled outside, the speck of dust jumped from his ear into the crow's skin.

The crow snatched the string from the baby's hand and took the ball of daylight high into the sky. The baby screamed so loudly that the chief and his daughter came running to see what was wrong. Hunters tried to bring the crow down with their arrows, but he was already beyond their reach.

The crow travelled westward, light from the swinging ball illuminated the ground below him. When he reached the land of the Inuit, he broke off a tiny piece of daylight as he flew over each village.

Reaching home at last, the crow dropped the ball so that it shattered into a hundred pieces and sent light shining into every house. The people were delighted and crowded around to thank him.

'If I had brought back the big daylight, there would never have been darkness here again,' the crow explained. 'There would have been light day and night, winter and summer. But the big daylight was too heavy for me to carry. I could only bring a small ball.'

That is why, it is said in the lands of the far North, it is dark for half of the year, and for the other half it is light. And why the Inuit have always been friends with the crow and never tried to kill him.

2

Nanook, the White Bear

*Story-telling was the only form of entertainment for the Inuit of
northern Canada during the long dark winters. In those days the
birth of twins was thought to be unlucky.
This story was told to a Frenchman who visited the Inuit during
the early years of this century.*

A long time ago, a woman gave birth to twin boys. The young
mother was very upset and her husband tried to comfort her.

'They are strong, healthy boys,' he said. 'Forget the stories
about twins being unlucky. Our babies will grow up to be good
hunters.'

But she would not be comforted. 'We will always have bad luck
while these children live,' she said. 'I have brought misfortune to
our family.'

The baby boys grew strong and became very hairy. When they
crawled across the fur rugs of the igloo, they could hardly be
seen, except for their gleaming, bright eyes.

This upset the young mother even more; her health was
affected and she could no longer give milk to feed them. One day
she took them out and abandoned them in the snow. Older
members of the family approved of her action. They thought this
should have been done when the babies were first born. The tribe
moved on and, in time, new people came into the district.

The babies did not die. Their strength and hairy skins saved
them. One twin crawled towards the sea with its great icebergs
and became Nanook, the white bear. The other baby struggled
towards the moss and bogs of the tundra and became Nanook,
the black bear. Meanwhile, everyone who knew about the twins
soon forgot them.

One day, a hunter called Uluksak was travelling across the
frozen sea when he heard the sound of cracking ice. The thaw
had set in early. Long widening gaps opened up between Uluksak

16

and the distant shore. He looked around desperately, but there was no path back to land. The unfortunate man was trapped on an ice floe and carried out to sea.

For days the hunter crouched on the swaying ice. The cold sapped his strength and, as he had eaten all his food, he pulled off his leather moccasins and started to chew them. Suddenly the ice floe tipped alarmingly and, looking around, Uluksak saw a white bear crawling out of the sea to join him. He lowered the moccasin from his lips. His heart sank. Now, for sure, he would be killed.

To his astonishment, the white bear gave a growl, more like a throaty purr than a snarl of attack. Then he spoke. 'Don't be afraid,' he said. 'I want to help you. I am a cousin of man, not his enemy.'

Seeing that Uluksak was starving, the white bear went hunting for fish. While the man ate, the bear lay at his side and warmed him with his fur and body heat. For several days these two unlikely friends shared the ice floe. Soon the food and warmth restored Uluksak's strength.

One morning the wind changed and the ice floe was blown back from the open sea. As the ice bumped against the shore, Uluksak said to his rescuer. 'I would like to tell my family about you, but nobody will believe me. Can you give me something to show the other Inuit?'

The bear thought for a moment, then he plucked some hairs

from the great clumps of fur that grew like boots all around his feet, and twisted them into a lace.

'Show this to your family,' he said. 'No man has ever made a lace like this. Only Nanook, the white bear and cousin to man, could have made such a lace.'

The great white bear dived into the sea. 'Goodbye, Uluksak,' he called as he swam away.

'Goodbye, Nanook,' replied Uluksak.

Then he went ashore to rejoin his family.

They were amazed and delighted to see him safely home but did not believe his story. 'You must have imagined it,' they said. 'Hunger made you see visions.'

Uluksak held out the lace that Nanook had woven from fur. None of them had ever seen such a thing before, and they could not tell how it had been made. Now his family believed him, and soon the whole tribe believed him.

More people examined the strange lace and no-one could discover how it had been made. At last everyone in the frozen North came to believe in the existence of Nanook, the white bear, the cousin of man.

3

Napi and the Buffalo-Stealer

Before the arrival of the white man, North America was populated by tribes of people who were thought to be of Asian origin. They were mostly hunter-gatherers, which means that they did not grow crops, and they lived very close to nature. The legends of the Blackfoot tribe were collected in the 1880s.

One year there was a great famine among the Blackfoot. The buffalo did not appear on the plains. The hunters hunted in vain and there was no meat for the cooking pots. First the old and the sick died, then the weak and the very young. When even the braves with their greater strength started to fall, the chief prayed to Napi, the great creator, for help.

Napi was far away in the sunny south, painting wing-feathers on the bright birds. But he heard the prayers and came at once to the Blackfoot lands.

The chief explained that the buffalo had not come grazing across the grasslands as they usually did and that his people were starving.

'Don't worry,' said Napi. 'I will find game for your hunters and look for the cause of the trouble.'

Napi took the chief's son with him and set off westwards in search of the buffalo. The two men travelled a long way before, on the other side of the green hills, they saw a small lodge by the side of a river. Napi stopped.

'Here is the cause of your trouble,' he said to the chief's son. 'A buffalo-stealer lives in that lodge. He has taken all the buffalo from the plains for himself and left nothing for anyone else.'

Then Napi turned himself into a pretty little dog and his companion into a fine, strong stick. The chief's son soon realised why. A little boy came running along the bank of the river.

'Oh, what a dear little dog,' he exclaimed. 'Let me keep it.'

The boy's mother, who adored him, agreed at once. She also

picked up the stick and said, 'We are in luck. This stick is exactly what I need for digging up roots.'

They walked together to the lodge of the buffalo-stealer, for they were his wife and son. Towards the end of the day, the buffalo-stealer returned home with buffalo meat for the pot. He glared at the little dog.

'I don't want that creature in the lodge,' he said. 'I don't like it. It has an evil look about it. It will do us no good.'

The little boy cried and said he loved the dog. The mother begged that the boy should not be upset and at last the buffalo-stealer agreed that the dog could stay. So the dog and the stick stayed while the meat was cooked for the evening meal. The family ate and then went to sleep.

When everything was quiet, Napi and the chief's son resumed their normal shapes and ate well from the cooked meat.

'This man has taken more buffalo than he can ever need. He is the cause of the trouble,' Napi said. 'In the morning you will see that I am right.'

In the morning the buffalo-stealer was furious that the meat had gone. 'It was that dog. He is evil. Get rid of him,' he yelled.

Once more the little boy cried and the woman pleaded, and the dog was allowed to stay. Presently the buffalo-stealer went out and, a little later, the woman picked up the stick and called the boy to come out to the bushes to look for roots and berries.

For half the morning, the woman dug for roots and the boy collected berries, while the dog frisked around them. Then the woman sat down to rest and put the stick on the ground at her side. The stick heard the little dog yapping from a thicket of bushes. Wriggling like a snake, the stick joined the dog, who was really Napi the great creator in disguise.

The dog had found a cave that was almost concealed by branches and brambles. Inside the cave were buffalo – herds and herds of buffalo that the buffalo-stealer had driven from the plains. The little dog ran in among the huge creatures and drove them out into the light. With the help of the stick, he began to drive the herds back towards the Blackfoot lands.

Suddenly the wife and son of the buffalo-stealer realised that the stick and the little dog were missing. Their cries brought back the buffalo-stealer. 'Where are my buffalo?' he shouted in a rage.

'We know nothing of your buffalo,' cried his wife and son, 'but our new stick and the dog have disappeared.'

'I knew that dog was evil,' roared the buffalo-stealer. 'He has taken the buffalo. I will find him and kill him and break the stick in two.'

Hearing these words from a great distance, Napi, still in the form of a dog, hid in the long mane of one of the buffalo and the stick crept in with him.

Although the buffalo-stealer raced to and fro, he could not see the dog or the stick and he could do

nothing to make the buffalo return to his cave. After several hours, when he felt safe from attack, Napi turned the stick back into the chief's son and assumed his own form again.

The Blackfoot people were overjoyed when they saw the buffalo being driven towards them across the plain. They built a paddock to keep some of the animals close to the village. But a huge, grey raven perched on the fence of the enclosure and frightened the buffalo away. The bird behaved in such a strange way that Napi became convinced that it was really the buffalo-stealer.

Napi turned himself into an otter and lay down near the grey bird, pretending to be dead. As the bird swooped down to make an easy meal, he seized the greedy creature by a leg. Resuming his normal shape again, Napi tied the huge grey bird over the smoke-hole of a wigwam. His feathers turned from grey to black and he coughed and choked until at last he begged for mercy.

'I confess I am the buffalo-stealer,' he cried, 'but release me or my wife and child will starve without me to hunt for them.'

Eventually Napi let the buffalo-stealer go. 'Hunt only what you need for your family,' he warned. 'If you take more, I will find you again and destroy you.'

The bird flew away and the Blackfoot tribe had no more trouble with the buffalo. From that day on, the feathers of the raven have been black and not grey.

4

The Medicine Wolf

One day the Blackfoot people were moving camp. They travelled in a slow-moving, straggling line, dragging their possessions on dog carts. The women, children and old people walked in the middle of the line, with the braves going on in front and bringing up the rear.

Suddenly a band of Crow warriors, who had been waiting in ambush, rushed out and attacked the centre of the line. They killed and robbed the travellers and took the stronger young women to be their slaves. Before the Blackfoot braves could reach the scene of the struggle, the attackers were away and could not be overtaken.

The Crow camp on the Yellowstone River was far from the scene of the ambush. The triumphant war party travelled for many days before they reached home with their exhausted prisoners.

One of the Blackfoot captives was a young woman called Sits-by-the-door. She was forced to work from dawn until dusk and was beaten if she refused. At night, the brave who had captured her tied her feet together and put another rope round her waist. He gave Sits-by-the-door to his wife.

The wife was not an unkind woman and felt sorry for the Blackfoot girl. Although their languages were different, she managed to speak a few words to the prisoner and, while her husband was out of camp, did her best to make life a little easier for the unfortunate slave.

One day, the wife told Sits-by-the-door that the braves were talking of killing her. 'You must escape tonight,' she said, 'or you will never see another sunset. I will help you.'

That night the wife waited until her husband's breathing told her that he was asleep. She crept over to Sits-by-the-door and untied the ropes. She gave her a new pair of moccasins, a flint and a small bag of pemmican cakes, which are a mixture of dried fruit and meat.

'Travel as far as you can before morning,' said the wife. 'When my husband and his friends find you are gone, they will follow you and, if they find you, they will kill you.'

Scarcely needing such advice, Sits-by-the-door hurried from the tepee and half walked and half ran until the sun was well above the horizon, and she knew that the Crow braves would be awake. Creeping into the thickest part of the undergrowth, she lay shivering with fear. She hoped that her efforts to walk on stony ground and leave no trail had succeeded.

She was lucky. Her captor and his friends searched for her for several hours but, when they found no tracks, they gave up and went home.

For four nights Sits-by-the-door walked towards the Blackfoot lands. During the day she hid and rested because she still feared that the Crow braves might be searching for her. She shivered with the cold, her moccasins wore out on the rough ground and she ate all the pemmican. Worst of all, she saw that she was being trailed by a large wolf. Desperately she tried to hurry and shake it off, but she was too weak and could only stumble along.

The wolf padded closer and closer, until one night he came and lay down at her side. Sits-by-the-door could scarcely breathe for terror, expecting at any moment to feel the wolf's sharp yellow teeth tearing at her throat. To her amazement, the wolf did not harm her, but lay close and kept her warm.

In the morning she said to him, 'I am faint for lack of food. If you cannot help me, I will die before I reach my home.'

The wolf looked at her with his sharp eyes and trotted away. He returned quickly and laid a freshly-killed buffalo calf at her feet. Sits-by-the-door started a fire with the flint given to her by the Crow woman and cooked some of the meat.

The food and warmth revived her and soon she was strong enough to continue the long walk home. Now she travelled by daylight with the wolf trotting a few paces behind her. By night she slept with the wolf at her side. When she was hungry, Sits-by-the-door rested in the undergrowth while the wolf hunted. Then they both ate.

At long last Sits-by-the-door walked into the camp of the Blackfoot people. How pleased they were to see her and how amazed they were to see a huge wolf walking at her heels. The children would have driven it out of the camp with sticks and stones, but Sits-by-the-door stopped them.

'He is my friend. He saved my life. There is powerful medicine between us,' she said. As the Indians believed in medicine, or magic, between humans and animals, the wolf was accepted into the camp and no-one harmed him.

For many months the wolf lived with Sits-by-the-door and fed in her lodge. But then Sits-by-the-door became ill and the village dogs drove the wolf out of the camp. Every evening the wolf would come to a hill and look down at the lodge where Sits-by-the-door lay sick. Her friends went out and threw food to him. Every evening the wolf came, until Sits-by-the-door breathed her last. Then, although the girl's friends went on throwing out food for him, the wolf was seen no more.

5

The Legend of Johnny Appleseed

The first Europeans in North America settled on the east coast. As their numbers grew, their eyes turned westwards. With the help of the Lord and a lot of hard work, they were convinced that they could make the wilderness blossom and live a life of freedom. Covered waggons filled with people began to roll into the unknown land.

Johnny Appleseed first saw the light of day at about the same time as the United States of America themselves – and that was quite a while ago. He lived over in the east, as did most of the folk in those times. Good people they were, too. They worked hard and read the Good Book and feared the Lord. They had built themselves some smart little towns, where the children could grow up decent, and outside the towns were plenty of real fine farms.

There were stories about forests and rivers and endless plains on the other side of the mountains to the west, but boys like Johnny Appleseed did not pay too much attention to them. Those wild places were for trappers and mountain men, not for families.

Johnny grew up to be an apple farmer. He owned row after row of apple trees that glowed with pink blossom in the springtime and were bowed down with shiny apples at summer's end. Johnny was proud of his apple trees, and everyone for miles around agreed that no one could raise apples like Johnny could.

Then one day, when he was not quite as young as he used to be, Johnny heard a rumbling and a creaking and a chattering and a clattering of hooves. He looked over his fence and saw a long line of covered waggons rolling along the track.

'Where might all you folk be going?' asked Johnny.

'We're going west,' they replied. 'We're going west where the forests are full of game and the rivers are full of fish and the land is black and rich and ready for farming, and where folk can make a new life and have room to grow.'

'Sounds mighty nice,' replied Johnny 'but are there any apple trees out west?'

'Reckon not,' laughed the people in the waggons.

'In that case I'm staying put right here,' grinned Johnny and went back to picking his apples.

Waggon after waggon rumbled along the track, throwing up so much dust that Johnny had to have a good cough. He looked over his fence once more.

'Landsakes! How many more of them are there?' he thought.

Then he saw that in one of the waggons was a gal he had been to school with, and clustered round her were her four rosy-cheeked little ones.

'Mary-Lou,' gasped Johnny. 'You surely aren't going to take those innocent children to a place where there aren't any apples! No apple pie! No apple dumplings! No crunchy apples to slip into their pockets when they sneak off a-fishing! What are you thinking of, Mary-Lou?'

Mary-Lou smiled at Johnny. 'We shall miss your apples, that's for sure, Johnny,' she said, 'but the west is the place for youngsters. It is the place where they can walk tall and free.'

'Don't see much fun in walking tall and free without an apple in your pocket,' muttered Johnny.

Mary-Lou called back to him, as she rolled away round the bend of the track, 'Fill your pockets with apple seeds, Johnny, and come west and plant apple trees for us. Then I can go on baking Momma's apple pie for the little ones.'

Johnny slipped down from the fence and sat in the orchard looking at his beloved apple trees. He did not want to leave his farm, but he felt real troubled about those fine folk setting off to start a new life in a land without apples.

It was the end of a hot day and Johnny had been working hard. He dozed in the shade and, with the buzzing of the insects and the distant rumbling of the waggon wheels, it seemed to him that an angel rustled out from among the leaves.

'Now look here, Johnny,' said the angel, 'that isn't the only waggon train heading west, you know, there's hundreds of them going. Now, how can you sit still and let all those good folk long for an apple, year in and year out, without so much as a sniff of one. You take your crop of apples and put all the seeds into a bag and head west. You plant apple seeds everywhere that looks a likely spot and you surely will be doing the work of the Lord.'

'Darn me, but I believe you're right,' said Johnny, and with that the angel disappeared.

Johnny didn't forget. Come the right time, which Johnny knew being a good apple farmer, he filled a bag with apple seeds and started walking west. He put his best spade on his shoulder, while on his head was a cooking pot that doubled as a hat. His cloak was made of an old coffee bag. In his jacket pockets were ribbons and little fancies to please the mothers and the children, and tucked in his inside pocket where it was safe from the rain, was the Bible, the Good Book itself.

'We all need the words of the Lord to guide us,' thought Johnny.

Johnny did not carry a gun and he was not afraid. 'I'm not a-going to hurt no one and no one ain't a-going to hurt me,' he smiled.

So Johnny walked west and he walked west and he walked west, until the towns and the apple orchards were left far behind him. Sometimes he slept under the stars, wrapped in his cloak. Sometimes he snuggled down among the dried leaves and undergrowth in the forests. Nothing ever harmed him, neither bear, nor snake, nor wolf, nor mountain lion. The wild creatures knew a good man when they saw one.

Wherever Johnny found a fertile spot of land where an apple tree could grow real good, he planted one of his apple seeds. He dug the soil over to make it easy for the young roots to wriggle downwards. He watered the new shoot and he built a fence around it to protect it until it was strong enough to look after itself. Then Johnny went marching on.

Sometimes, as darkness fell, Johnny would see the lights of a cabin where some of the folk from the waggon trains had liked the look of the land and dropped off to make a garden in the wilderness. Then Johnny would go a-knocking at the door and ask if there was a mite of supper to spare, if all the family had already eaten their fill. Then, while the good lady of the family was filling a plate for him, Johnny would take out a pretty ribbon and give it to the little girl of the house. And mighty pleased she would be, as it was probably the first pretty ribbon she had ever seen in her life.

When he had eaten his supper and said his thank yous, Johnny would take out his Bible and ask the folk if they would like him to read to them from the Good Book.

'Can you read?' they would gasp, for there wasn't much schooling about in an empty wilderness and folk who could read were thin on the ground.

'Sure can,' Johnny would grin. And he would sit and read all evening to the family, who gathered round real grateful for the children to hear such fine words.

Then before he left next morning, Johnny would plant a little orchard of apple trees at the side of the farm, and tell the folk how to care for the growing trees.

'This is a job for you,' he would say to the little boys. 'You tend these trees real good like I'm telling you and before you can look round, you'll be carrying apples in to your Ma and asking her to bake you deep-plate apple pies, just like Grandma used to make.'

'Thank you, Johnny. We'll do as you say,' the little boys would reply.

And the little fellows were as good as their word. Everywhere

that Johnny had visited, everywhere that he had stopped in the forest, apple trees sprang up. In the springtime, as folk looked out across a valley or over the plain, they would see a path of apple blossom.

'That's the way Johnny Appleseed walked,' they would smile. 'Good old Johnny Appleseed.'

The years went by and apple trees were everywhere. Now there was not so much need for Johnny and his apple seeds, but still he walked the trails, stopping at a farm here and calling at an apple festival there. He was always welcome.

In fact he was more than welcome. As soon as people saw who it was, Johnny Appleseed was made the chief guest. At harvest time, when the locals gathered to help each other with the apple picking and to enjoy a picnic and dancing, Johnny Appleseed would be sat at the top of the table and given a plate piled high with food.

'There would be no apples without Johnny Appleseed,' laughed the farmers. 'Good luck to Johnny, who gave us our apple pies and apple dumplings and toffee apples.'

Then Johnny would smile and eat a little of the food, for he never ate a lot, and go on his way.

One year Johnny lay down to rest in a forest and suddenly there was a rustling of leaves and that same angel, who had spoken to him so many years ago in the old apple orchard, came and stood before him.

'Time for you to come with me, Johnny,' the angel said. 'The Good Lord is waiting for you.'

'I can't go yet,' gasped Johnny. 'I've still got a few apple seeds to plant.'

'Well, you can't plant them down here,' said the angel, 'but I tell you what, there's a corner in the garden of the Lord where we could do with some new trees.'

'In that case, I don't mind going with you,' said Johnny. And putting his hand into that of the angel, he left all worldly cares behind.

6

Pilotte, the Dog that Saved a Colony

Canada is the icy crown of the North American continent. It stretches from the south of the Arctic Circle down to the lush market gardens next to the border with the United States of America. Many immigrants have come to this vast land.
This story concerns some men and women who made the long journey from France, and a dog that came to their rescue.

Immigrants to a new land will always look for the greenest pastures and the best hunting grounds in which to settle. But when they stake their claim in their sunny new homelands, they do not always consider that, if the location is so good, someone else may have found it before them.

So it was with the small band of French settlers who arrived on the island of Montreal over three hundred years ago. They saw the clean river water, the forests that offered a free larder of game and the lush grass on which to feed their domestic animals. To European eyes, accustomed to the tamed and densely-populated landscapes of their old homes, the new country seemed empty of people.

But it was not!

The Iroquois people were already hunting across that landscape and saw no reason why they should make room for newcomers.

The French settlers felled trees and built a sturdy fort and a hospital. They put up an altar and Father Vimont, their priest, prayed that their little settlement would grow and one day would be a fine city.

A few weeks after their arrival, most of the men were down by the river, clearing land and cutting more timber. Suddenly a screeching war-cry split the still air and a band of Iroquois braves on horseback charged into the clearing. Before the settlers could reach the safety of the fort, they were savagely attacked. The lucky ones were killed in the fighting. No one cared to think about the lingering deaths of the others.

Inside the fort it was safe. The settlers carried on trading and farming and welcomed newcomers from France to swell their numbers.

But they had to be constantly on guard. Sentries kept watch day and night and anyone thoughtless enough to become separated from his companions was usually found dead. The Iroquois harassed and robbed them, until the settlers started to discuss leaving the island.

Paul de Chomedy was one of the original settlers. He did not wish to leave because it seemed disloyal to those who had died. He had the idea of sending back to Paris for a supply of dogs.

The right dogs could save this settlement, he thought. The right dogs would be able to tell the difference between Iroquois and other men. They could be trained to patrol the forest and give us warning of an attack.

So a request for dogs was sent to France. This commission, to supply dogs to a village on an island half a world away, did not seem very urgent or important to the agents in Paris.

Other, more profitable orders were attended to. Then, shortly before the next supply ship was due to sail, they remembered the order for the dogs. Hastily a pack of strays was rounded up from the streets of Paris. Old and young, big and small—if the dog had no obvious owners, it joined the shipment to Montreal.

After a rough voyage across the Atlantic in a wooden sailing ship, the rowdy dogs were loaded into small boats for the journey to Montreal Island.

Paul de Chomedy welcomed the dogs ashore eagerly, but they were not quite what he had hoped for. Some were sick and soon died. Others had lived wild for too long and

35

could not be trained. Many had vicious natures, which was why they had been turned out on the streets in the first place. None of them seemed intelligent enough to learn the difference between the scents of an Iroquois, a Frenchman and a member of a friendly tribe.

There was only one suitable dog among the mongrel pack. She was a female with a fine sense of smell and a faithful nature. The settlers called her Pilotte.

Pilotte patrolled the edges of the forest. She could pick up the scent of an Iroquois and never confused it with the trails of Frenchmen or friendly tribesmen. When she padded across the tracks of an Iroquois, or spotted one moving between the trees, Pilotte would rush back to the fort, barking to raise the alarm. The Iroquois warriors found that attacking the settlers and stealing from the encampment became more and more difficult.

Pilotte bore several litters of pups and trained them to patrol in the same way. Soon relays of fine dogs guarded the forest tracks.

In 1648 a man named Lambert Closse was sent to Montreal to organise proper defences for the settlement.

Pilotte came forward to snuffle a greeting to the new defender of her territory. From that first moment she and Lambert Closse were friends. Pilotte walked watchfully at Lambert's heels as he surveyed the forest approaches and made plans. Soon the Iroquois attacks ceased and, before much longer, they were only a fading memory. So, from a tragic beginning, the settlement on Montreal Island grew into a lovely city.

The modern citizens of Montreal, living in their warm houses and rolling along smooth roads in comfortable motor cars, have not forgotten the desperate struggles of days gone by. The fine monument in the Place d'Armes is a tribute to the city's founding fathers. On the base of the monument is a carved figure of a dog. It is Pilotte.

7

Paul Bunyan

The United States of America is a young country, freshly hewn from the wilderness by determined men eager to build a new nation. Paul Bunyan was one of those men.

The big forest was no place for small men. If roads were to reach into the wilderness, those trees had to be felled. If houses were to be built to shelter the new settlers, those trees had to be felled. If railroads were to join the east coast to the west, those trees had to be felled. But those trees had hides tougher than buffalo and the earth shook when they hit the ground. It took a special breed of men to topple those giants of the forest. If men were tall in Texas, they had to be tough in timber country.

Legend tells us that the toughest, strongest lumberjack who ever lifted an axe, was Paul Bunyan. Paul was remarkable from the day he was born. He was a big, strong, bonny baby and his folks were proud of him. Of course he was a mite of trouble. He was too big for the cradle which had fitted the other babies and his Pa had to set to and build a new one, and that was only the start of it.

When Paul grew big enough to laugh and clap his hands, the vibration broke every pane of glass in the house. In the end Paul's Pa grew tired of replacing the glass and left the window frames empty for the breeze to blow in and out as it liked.

However that was nothing to what happened when young Paul was big enough to run around the village and play. Every time he sneezed or coughed loudly, he blew the roofs off the nearest houses. After it had happened three or four times, some of the folks went to Paul's Pa and complained. Mighty mean, some people are!

Then, when Paul had grown into quite a lad, he decided it was time to learn to swim. He went down to the sea and jumped in, and he made a splash so big that a tidal wave flooded the land for miles around.

'Pa!' said Paul's Mom. 'If we don't watch out, that boy of ours will soon be getting difficult!'

In the spring when the loggers went up into the forests,

Paul's Pa, who was a logger, took Paul with him. Paul was taught which trees to fell for building houses, which trees were best for laying railroads, and which trees were best for furniture-making. He was taught how to fell a tree, where to fell a tree, at what age to fell a tree, and where to sell a tree. Paul's Pa was a good teacher and Paul was a good learner.

By the end of that first summer, there was nothing about trees that Paul did not know.

The next summer he set up a camp of his own. Paul swung his axe and felled trees until the axe became red hot. Folks gathered round and warmed their hands at it.

Paul Bunyan's name and fame spread all through the forest. Other tough lumberjacks came to join him. They wanted to see if they could outchop the famous Paul, but no one ever could. Paul was such a fine fellow and such a fair boss that all the good loggers stayed with him. His camp became the most successful in the forest and his men lived in the warmest cabins and ate the best food and made the most money. Paul was smart as well as tough.

Of course, Paul did have his strange ways. Most loggers had a dog for a pet, if they had a pet. Not Paul. Paul Bunyan's pet was a blue ox!

One winter, so the story goes, some mighty strange snow fell over the forest. The snow was blue. Some folks said the blue of the sky had stuck to it as it came down. Others laughed and said the blue was the minerals washing up out of the rivers. Whichever way it was, as he was walking past a big blue snowdrift, Paul Bunyan saw a baby ox calf lost and half frozen. He picked him up and carried him home. No one knew if the little creature was blue from the snow or blue from the cold, but blue he was and blue he stayed for the rest of his life. Paul called him Babe and made him his pet.

Babe was like his master. He was big. First he drank eighteen pints of milk a day. Soon he was drinking eighteen gallons. After that folk stopped counting.

Babe also grew well. To begin with he lived in the dog kennel.

Then he moved to the wood shed. Next he had to find bigger quarters in the barn – and that was all on his first day! Babe was happy in the barn for some time. Then one morning Paul looked out of his bedroom window and saw that his barn had gone. He ran outdoors and looked across the fields. Feeding in one field was a huge blue ox. It was Babe. 'Babe is thriving well. I have a fine animal there!' smiled Paul. 'But what is that strange sort of wooden saddle he seems to have on his back?'

He looked again and saw that the saddle was his barn. Babe had grown so big that he had walked away with the whole barn on his back.

After that Babe was taken to live at the logging camp. Worth his weight in gold he was. With his huge strength, the mighty animal dragged cut timber to the river and moved huts from one part of the mountain to the other.

Then, one summer, Paul Bunyan had a real problem. There was a fine stand of special trees needed felling for a rich customer who would pay a top price. Cutting the trees was easy for Paul, but getting them down to the river was difficult. Only one twisty road ran from the mountainside down to the valley. It was clear to everyone that those tall fine trees would never get round the bends in that road.

'Babe!' said Paul. 'It's time you earned those sugar-lumps I give you of a Saturday night!'

Then Paul put a harness round Babe's shoulders and hitched him to one end of that twisty road.

'Pull, Babe!' ordered Paul. Babe pulled and heaved and pawed the ground. It was a tough task and Babe sweated a tiny bit but, with one last lunge forward, Babe pulled the whole road straight.

After that Paul took the trees down to the valley with no

trouble at all. 'Things are easy when you know how to set about them,' he grinned.

Now Paul was not merely big and tough, he was smart. One day he fell to thinking about the way he ran his lumber camp.

'I reckon as I'm a-wasting money up here,' he said. 'I'm spending money on things we don't need, that could be spent on good things like extra beans with our beef, and more syrup on our pancakes.'

Paul spoke to his friend Johnny Inkslinger, who kept all the books for the buying and selling of the timber. By this time Paul's camp was so big and so successful that Johnny Inkslinger was using ink by the barrelful. He used so much that he had a hose fitted from the barrels to his pen, so that he did not have to get up each time his fountain pen needed refilling.

'Johnny,' said Paul. 'We are going to save money on ink.'

'How can that be, with all the orders and bills and receipts I have to write?' asked Johnny.

'Well,' replied Paul. 'From now on, stop dotting "i"s and crossing "t"s. It isn't necessary. Everyone will still understand what you mean.'

'Dang me, if you may not be right!' agreed Johnny Inkslinger.

He stopped dotting 'i's and crossing 't's and in a few weeks, he had saved six barrels of ink. The money gained was put to good use and all the loggers said what a fine thing it was to work for a smart boss.

The stories about Paul Bunyan are endless. They could fill a book on their own, but here our tale must end. Some folk say that Paul is still out there in the distant hills felling trees. That may not be true. It sounds like rather a tall story, and telling a tall story would never do!

8

The Fate of Napoleon

This strange story was told by Chief Capilano of the Squamish people, who visited London in 1906. Although in places the story appears to have gained in the telling, parts of it have a ring of truth, particularly the account of the French prisoners. It certainly shows how news can travel the world in unexpected ways.

During the late eighteenth century, the Pacific coast of Canada was very remote from Europe. It would seem very unlikely that any of the Indian tribes living there could have heard of the French commander, Napoleon Bonaparte. But they had. They called him the 'Great French Fighter' and took a close interest in his fate.

Hunters who explored the lonely reaches of the far north, were not surprised that the tribes living near Quebec should have a knowledge of French affairs. French immigrants had settled there over a century before. However, when they reached the far shores of the Pacific, the hunters were puzzled to find a demand for the latest news about Napoleon.

'Have you had other travellers here from Quebec?' asked the hunters. 'Did they tell you about France?'

'No! No!' the natives replied. 'Our news came from the west.'

To the west was the Pacific Ocean, so the hunters were mystified.

Later, in the days of Edward VII of England, Chief Capilano of the Squamish people travelled to London to promise loyalty to the English king. While he was there he told the story of 'The Lost Talisman'. He claimed that this loss had sealed the fate of Napoleon, the 'Great French Fighter'.

In those days, the warriors of the Squamish tribe liked to carry a talisman, or protective charm. This was always a bone from the spine of a sea-serpent. The bigger and more magical the sea-serpent had been, the more powerful was the talisman.

Sea-serpents were rare and terrifying creatures. Anybody who approached one was instantly bewitched as though he had gone out of his mind. Legs and arms became disjointed with fits of shaking or paralysis. Only a warrior of complete and absolute purity could overcome a sea-serpent.

When a spine of one of these fearsome monsters fell into human hands, it had to be treated with great caution. Medicine men used the power of their magic over each bone of the spine so that it did not harm its wearer, but his enemies were afflicted by dreadful seizures.

Now it so happened that one of these bone talismans had been for many years the treasured possession of a Squamish warrior, the hero of many battles. When the day came for this man to die, he had no close male relative to whom he could pass on the powerful charm. The family who wept at his deathbed were sisters, daughters and grand-daughters – but no men.

This greatly distressed the old man because he knew the talisman must not be kept by a woman. He wanted the powerful charm to help another great warrior, so before he died, he made the women promise to send the talisman to the 'Great French Fighter' called Napoleon Bonaparte'.

The old women of the family said it was impossible to send the charm to Napoleon and thought that it should be buried with the dead man. But the younger women would not agree. They were determined to fulfil the last wishes of the fine old warrior. They kept the talisman safe and turned their eyes towards the sea.

The very next day, a Russian seal-hunting ship sailed in and anchored in their inlet. The Squamish people had learned about Europe from visitors such as these.

The sailors came ashore and spoke with another white man, who was a trapper down from Hudson's Bay.

Later the women asked him if the sailors knew of Napoleon.

'You are in luck,' replied the trapper. 'Did you notice those two men who are different in appearance? The two thinner, taller men who do not mix with the others?'

The Squamish women had noticed the men, who had been badly treated by the rest of the crew and appeared to be little better than slaves.

'They are Frenchmen,' explained the trapper. 'They are prisoners and are being forced to work for the Russians. Perhaps they can give you news of Napoleon.'

The women waited for an opportunity to speak to the two Frenchmen. They asked them to take the sea-serpent's bone to the 'Great French Fighter'.

At first the two men were reluctant. 'How do we know we will ever return to France?' they asked. 'And if this talisman is so powerful, will it not affect us? We are not of your tribe.'

The women assured the two men that no harm would come to them. 'The medicine man has put a spell on it,' they said. 'If we give it to you freely, it will not harm you. It will bring trouble only to your enemies.'

At last the Frenchmen were persuaded to take the talisman. When the sealing ship had been serviced and restocked, it pushed out into midstream and headed for the open sea. The Squamish women stood on the banks of the inlet to watch it leaving. Then they saw a strange sight. All the Russians on deck started to fall about and clutch their heads. They were being attacked by fits of the palsy. Only the two Frenchmen were unaffected by the seizures. By the time the ship reached the open sea, the Frenchmen were in charge. Then the vessel was lost to sight.

In later years other ships brought back news of what had happened. Once they were the owners of a fine little ship, the Frenchmen were able to make their way back to their homeland. Then, full of gratitude for the good luck given to them by the Squamish talisman, they went to Napoleon and gave him the bone from the sea-serpent.

From that moment on Napoleon won even greater victories. His enemies fell before him, confused and helpless. This continued for several years until, one terrible day, Napoleon mislaid the talisman.

Chief Capilano looked round at his spellbound listeners. 'It

happened when the great Emperor was on his way to do battle with people of your tribe.' he said. 'He was about to fight the English.'

'What was the name of the battle, do you know?' asked one of the listeners.

'Yes, yes,' said Chief Capilano. 'It was a hard name for an Indian to say and in my land, we had almost forgotten it. But since I have been in London, I have heard the name several times. You have given the same name to a railway station. The name we heard from visiting sailors over on the Pacific coast was Waterloo. They said Napoleon had fought a great battle with the English at Waterloo and that he had been defeated. He was defeated because he had lost the charm sent to him by the Squamish people.'

News of great events travels to the remote parts of the world in the strangest ways.

9

The Moon in the Millpond

The adventures of Brer Rabbit and his rascally friends were first written down by an American journalist named Joel Chandler Harris, who was born in 1848. Harris grew up in the southern state of Georgia. He used to visit the cabins where the black slaves lived and listen to the fireside stories told by the old men. Later, when he was writing a daily column for a newspaper in Atlanta, Georgia, Harris remembered his boyhood days and retold one of the stories he had heard about Brer Rabbit. It was an immediate success. From then on stories about the doings of Brer Rabbit and his friends, recounted by an old character named Uncle Remus, were a regular feature of the newspaper. They have been popular ever since.

Many years ago a little boy used to visit an old man named Uncle Remus to listen to the tales he told about that scamp, Brer Rabbit, and Brer Fox, and all the other folk and animals who lived in the olden days.

One day the little boy found Uncle Remus sitting in his usual chair and talking about a time when all the animals had been at peace with each other.

'Tell me about that,' said the little boy.

So Uncle Remus settled himself comfortably and began.

There was a time when there had been no trouble for weeks and weeks. All the animals chatted and talked together as if there had never been any falling out. Now that Brer Rabbit, he began to feel bored. He lay in the sun and kicked at the gnats. Then he nibbled at the grass. And finally he rolled in the sand.

Then he fell in with Brer Terrapin and, after they had shaken hands, they sat down by the side of the road and chatted about old times. By and by Brer Rabbit ventured to say that he thought it was time to stop being peaceful and have some fun.

'Brer Rabbit,' said Brer Terrapin, 'you're just the fellow I've been looking for.'

'Well then,' said Brer Rabbit, 'we'll tell Brer Fox and Brer Wolf and Brer Bear that tomorrow night we'll meet them down by the millpond to do a little fishing.'

Brer Rabbit paused. 'I'll do all the talking. All you have to do is to sit back and say "Yes. That's right, Brer Rabbit".'

With that Brer Rabbit ran off home and went to bed.

Now Brer Terrapin, he was rather slow at getting about, so he set off for the millpond to make sure that he would be there on time. Next day Brer Rabbit sent word to all the other animals about going fishing in the millpond that night.

'How wonderful,' they all said. 'Why didn't we think of that?'

Brer Fox invited Miss Meadows and Miss Motts to come and watch how clever he was at fishing. In those days animals dressed in clothes and talked to human beings.

Sure enough, when the time came, everyone was at the millpond. Brer Bear brought a hook and line. Brer Wolf brought a hook and line. Brer Fox brought a dip net and, not to be outdone, Brer Terrapin brought the bait.

Miss Meadows and Miss Motts didn't bring anything. They stood well back from the edge of the pond and squealed every time Brer Terrapin shook the bait box at them.

Brer Bear said he was going to fish for mudcats. Brer Wolf said he was going to fish for horney-heads. Brer Fox said he was going to fish for perch for the ladies. Brer Terrapin said he was going to fish for minnows. Brer Rabbit winked at Brer Terrapin and said he was going to fish for suckers.

They all got ready and Brer Rabbit marched up to the pond and made as if to throw his line into the water. Suddenly it seemed as if he saw something. The other animals stopped and watched. Brer Rabbit dropped his fishing rod. He stood there scratching his head and looking down into the water.

The girls began to feel uneasy and Miss Meadows, she shouted out, 'Landsakes, Brer Rabbit! What in the name of goodness is the matter in there?'

But Brer Rabbit, he just scratched his head and looked into the water.

Miss Motts, she hitched up her skirts and said she was monstrous feared of snakes and she surely hoped there were no snakes about.

Brer Rabbit, he kept on scratching his head and looking into

that millpond. 'Ladies and gentlemen,' he said, 'we might as well make tracks for home. There's going to be no fishing in this pond.'

With that Brer Terrapin, he scrambled up to the edge of the pond and looked over. He shook his head and said, 'Yes. That's right, Brer Rabbit.'

Then Brer Rabbit called out to the girls, 'Don't worry, ladies. We'll take care of you. There's nothing much the matter except that the moon has dropped into the water.'

With that they all went to the bank and looked in. Sure enough, there lay the moon, a-swinging and a-swaying at the bottom of the pond.

Brer Fox, he looked in and said, 'Well, well, well!'

Brer Wolf, he looked in and said, 'Mighty bad! Mighty bad!'

Brer Bear, he looked in and said, 'Tum, tum, tum!'

The ladies looked in and Miss Meadows, she squealed out, 'Well, I never did!'

Brer Rabbit spoke up, 'Ladies and gentlemen, whatever you say, unless we get that moon out of the pond, there will be no fish caught this night. Ask Brer Terrapin, he will tell you the same.'

And Brer Terrapin, he said, 'Yes. That's right, Brer Rabbit.'

Then the other animals asked how they could get the moon out of the millpond.

Now Brer Rabbit, he looked at Brer Terrapin and said, 'I reckon the best way out of this little difficulty is to send round to your old uncle, Mr Mud-Turtle. We'll borrow his big net with the handles and drag that old moon out of the millpond.'

And Brer Terrapin, he said, 'Yes. That's right, Brer Rabbit.'

All the animals agreed that Brer Rabbit should go and borrow the net from Uncle Mud-Turtle.

While he was gone, Brer Terrapin said that he had heard tell, time and again, that anyone who pulled the moon from the water pulled a pot of money out with it. This made Brer Fox and Brer Wolf and Brer Bear feel mighty good and they said that, as Brer Rabbit had been so kind as to fetch the net, they would do the fishing for the moon.

When Brer Rabbit got back with the net, he made as if he wanted to go into the water. He pulled off his coat and was just unbuttoning his waistcoat, when the other animals said they wouldn't dream of letting Brer Rabbit go into the water.

So Brer Fox, he took hold of one handle of the net and Brer Wolf, he took hold of the other handle and Brer Bear, he waded along behind them to lift the big net clear of logs and snags.

They made one haul, but they didn't get the moon.

They made another haul – still no moon.

By and by, they got further out from the bank. Water ran into Brer Fox's ear. He shook his head. Water ran into Brer Wolf's ear. He shook his head. Water ran into Brer Bear's ear. He shook his head. And while they were a-shaking their heads and before they knew what was happening, they came to where the bottom of the pond shelved down fast.

Brer Fox, he stepped into deep water. Brer Wolf, he stepped into deep water. Brer Bear, he stepped into deep water. And goodness gracious, they kicked and splattered so much, it seemed as if they would splash all the water out of the pond.

When they finally scrambled out, the girls were a-sniggering and a-giggling and no wonder, for look where you might, you would never see three sillier-looking creatures than Brer Wolf, Brer Fox and Brer Bear.

Brer Rabbit, he shouted out, 'I expect you gentlemen will want to go home and put on dry clothes.' He grinned. 'Better luck next time. I do hear say that the moon will bite at a hook if you have fools for bait.'

So Brer Fox and Brer Wolf and Brer Bear went dripping away. Brer Rabbit and Brer Terrapin went off for a party with the girls.

Uncle Remus looked at the little boy, 'Time for you to go home, too,' he said.

South America

10

The Earth Giants

The Central American countries of Mexico and Guatemala often have earthquakes and this is reflected in their folklore. The Aztec people were very powerful before Columbus arrived. Their book, Popul Vuh (or Book of Leaves), tells how they thought the world began and who caused the earthquakes. The Popul Vuh was lost for many years and then rediscovered in the University of San Carlos, Guatemala in 1854.

Hurakan, the mighty wind god, blew through the universe and created the earth. He was the mother and the father of the gods. He made the animals. Then he created humans from corn cobs. However, the humans became disrespectful and insolent to the gods, who decided to destroy them.

The gods sent torrents of rain and a surging flood swept across the earth. They made the animals turn against the humans and attack them. When people climbed onto the roofs of houses to escape, the gods made the houses crumble. When they scrambled to the tops of trees, the gods made the trees fall down. Even the mountains offered no shelter, because the caves clanged shut against them. So all the humans were destroyed, leaving only their little cousins, the monkeys, in the trees.

For many years the earth struggled to recover from this devastation. Then the gods sent a few bands of humans to tame the wilderness and make the world a pleasant place again. Before this task finished, two giants came to live in the mountains of Mexico. They were called Zipacna and Cabrakan. Every day Zipacna piled up mountains and every day his brother, Cabrakan, shook them with earthquakes.

The brothers were boastful and proud and the gods did not like them. Hun-Apu and Xbalanque, the heavenly twins, were sent down to earth with orders to crush the destructive giants.

Hun-Apu and Xbalanque gathered together a band of four hundred young men. They went to a part of the forest through which Zipacna always walked on his way to the mountains. The young men cut down a huge tree and then waited for the giant to pass by.

'Why have you cut down that tree?' Zipacna asked in his huge booming voice as soon as he saw the men.

'We want to use it as the roof beam of a house we are building,' they replied.

'And can you not lift it, you miserable little creatures?' thundered the giant.

'No, we cannot. We are not as strong as you are,' said the young men.

Glad to find an opportunity to show off his strength, Zipacna lifted the huge tree on to his shoulder.

'Show me where you wish to build your house,' he said to the men, 'and I will take the tree there.'

He strode through the forest behind them until they came to a deep ditch. The men told Zipacna that the ditch was for the foundations of their house, and persuaded him to climb into it. When the giant was on his hands and knees, they threw tree trunks and boulders on him, hoping to kill him.

Zipacna realised what was happening and took cover in a side tunnel that the men had planned to use as a cellar underneath the house. When they saw no movement underneath the trees and boulders, the men thought they had killed the giant. They began to sing and dance with triumph.

To convince them that he was dead, Zipacna pulled several hairs from his head and gave them to some ants to take up to the surface.

'Tell the men you took these from my dead body,' said the giant, and the ants obeyed him.

The men were now convinced that Zipacna was dead. They built a great house over the ditch. Then they took food and drink

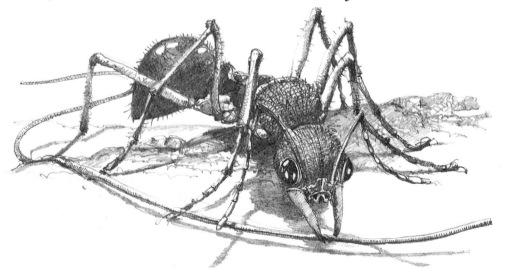

into the new building and held a party. For hours the house rang with singing and laughter. However, while Zipacna had been lying in the cellar, he had been building up his strength and plotting revenge.

Suddenly he stood up and threw the house and everyone in it high into the air. The building was destroyed and the young men were thrown so far into the sky that they never came down. They remained in the heavens and were changed into the stars that we call the Pleiades.

Hun-Apu and Xbalanque were dismayed that the band of young men had been defeated. This time they were determined to destroy the giant themselves. They watched Zipacna for several days and saw that he liked to eat crabs, which he collected from a river at the foot of a certain mountain.

The heavenly twins made a model of a large, delicious-looking crab and put it in the river at the foot of the mountain. Then they hollowed out the mountain and waited.

Soon Zipacna came wandering along the riverside.

'What are you looking for?' called Hun-Apu.

'If it is any of your business,' thundered Zipacna, 'I am looking for crabs and fish to eat for my dinner.'

'Then look down there,' advised Xbalanque, the other heavenly twin, pointing to the deepest ravine of the river. 'Only a few moments ago, I saw a crab big enough even for a giant like you.'

As Zipacna splashed down into the depths of the river, Hun-Apu and Xbalanque threw the mountain on top of him.

Zipacna was so strong that, even with so many tons of rock on his back, it looked as if he might break free. The heavenly twins saw the earth heaving and tumbling and quickly used their magic powers to turn Zipacna into stone. To this day, a huge stone that was once the giant Zipacna lies at the foot of Mount Meahuan near Vera Paz.

The heavenly twins' task was not yet completed. Cabrakan, the brother of Zipacna, still walked about the earth, shouting and boasting and shaking the mountains. He terrorised everyone who lived there. So Hun-Apu and Xbalanque set out to confront the terrible giant.

'Good morning,' they said cheerfully. 'Who are you and what do you do?'

'I am the great Cabrakan,' he boomed. 'I can pick up or throw down any mountain you care to mention. Let me show you.'

'Oh yes, indeed,' agreed the heavenly twins. 'But surely you need a meal to build up your strength before you perform such wonderful feats? Can we help by hunting some birds with our blow pipes and preparing them for your dinner?'

'If you like,' agreed the giant. He watched while Hun-Apu and Xbalanque shot two birds out of the sky. He would have been happy to eat them raw, but the heavenly twins insisted on covering them with clay and roasting them over a fire.

'They taste so much better cooked this way,' they insisted. They had put poison into the clay and this soaked into the skins of the birds.

When the birds were cooked through and smelled delicious, the twins handed them to Cabrakan. He swallowed them in huge, vulgar gulps.

'Now I will show you how to topple a mountain,' he boasted. But as he stood up, the poison ran through his veins.

He rubbed his hand across his eyes. 'I cannot see so well today,' he sighed.

As he took a step towards the mountains he fell to his knees. 'Where has my strength gone?' he asked.

Then he felt cold… and he shivered… and he collapsed on the ground.

So it was that the last of the Earth Giants died and Hun-Apu and Xbalanque, the heavenly twins, returned to live with the gods.

11

How the Moon Was Made

Before the Europeans came to South America, folk tales were not written down. Records were kept by tying knots in variously coloured pieces of string. Legends were passed on by word of mouth.
Any folk tales that have survived from the early days were recorded by Europeans after their arrival. The explorers of the late nineteenth and early twentieth centuries, when writing accounts of their adventures, also sometimes recorded the legends of the tribes they were visiting.

Back in the time when the world was young, Mair was the god of the sun. Every day he travelled across the sky from east to west. Every night he travelled under the earth and came up again on the other side. Sometimes Mair took the form of a jaguar. Sometimes he took the form of a snake. Jaguars and snakes were always his helpers and travelled with him through the underworld. However, there was no light at night while Mair was in the underworld because there was no moon in those days.

One day a man of the Urubu tribe became the father of a son. He held a feast for his relatives to choose a name for the boy, so that he could then be offered as a servant to Mair, the sun god. The feast began at sunset with much eating and drinking. The father hoped that by dawn everyone would have agreed on a name for the newborn boy.

However, one man and one woman would not stay and pay proper attention to the serious business of choosing a name. They ran away into a hut and the woman painted the man's face. She put big black circles round his eyes, a black line down his nose and a black mark across his mouth. They talked and giggled and took no notice of the other members of the family who were searching for them.

At last, as dawn came, the man and woman remembered their

duty and went out into the light of day to help to choose the name for the new baby. The man suddenly remembered the marks that the woman had painted on his face. He tried to wash them off before the others saw them but, no matter how much he rinsed his face, the black marks would not go. His relatives jeered at him when they saw the ridiculous marks.

Neither the man with the marks on his face, nor the woman who had painted them, were allowed to join in the final ceremonies for choosing the name of the baby, and they were turned away from the remainder of the feasting.

Suddenly the man snatched up an armful of arrows and a bow and ran to a big clearing in the jungle. The woman ran after him. The man pulled the bow string back as far as he could and shot an arrow high into the sky. It flew so high that it could not fall down. The man shot another arrow that hit the butt of the first one and it also stayed in the sky. Then the man shot another and another.

At last he had shot so many arrows that they stretched down to earth like a ladder. He threw away his bow and climbed up the ladder of arrows, wishing to go away and hide his black-marked face. The woman, not wanting to be left on earth and be blamed by her relatives for the trouble she had caused, climbed the ladder of arrows after the man. They disappeared into the sky and were lost to their family forever.

Three days later the Urubu people saw a pale light in the night sky. It was not bright and burning like the blaze of Mair in the daytime. It was silver and faint. The tribesmen were looking for the first time at the moon. It was a crescent new moon but, as the month wore on, it grew full and round. On its face the watching tribesmen saw the same black marks around the eyes, the nose and the mouth as had been on the face of their relative who had climbed up the ladder of arrows.

'There is our brother who has become the moon,' they said. 'There is his face as it was painted here on earth.'

Then they noticed a bright star that followed the moon in its travels over the sky.

'There is the woman who followed our brother,' said the Urubu. 'She has been turned into a star and is forever following the moon, seeking to wipe the black marks from his face.'

From that time on, Mair the sun travelled across the sky by day. At night the darkness was lit by the moon with its black-marked face and the bright star that followed it.

12

Jungle Spirits

As all the tribesmen of the Amazon basin know, the jungle is full of spirits. Most of the spirits are evil and need to be treated with respect and caution or, best of all, avoided.

Curupir is the owner of the jungle and a powerful spirit. His feet are turned back to front, so that his footprints are deceptive. Those who thought they were running away from Curupir were actually running towards him and could easily be captured. Curupir was a great friend of the tortoises and anyone who went tortoise hunting had to be very careful.

One day a hunter went into the jungle and caught several tortoises. He set up camp, lit a fire and cooked a tortoise for his supper. As the hunter settled down to sleep, he heard a noise approaching: 'Te-wo-yi! Te-wo-yi!! TE-WO-YI!!!'

The noise came closer and became louder. The terrified hunter leapt to his feet. Limping towards him through the trees, he saw a tall creature with swollen knees. A calabash was tied around each leg. The clashing of the calabashes made the eerie 'te-wo-yi' noise. Around the creature's neck hung some more calabashes, and these gave out a weird green light.

The hunter knew at once who his visitor was. It was the spirit Timakana, the friend of Curupir. The hunter screamed with fright. 'Go away!' he shouted. 'Go away and leave me alone.'

Still the figure stood in the bushes near the fire, staring at the hunter with burning red eyes, but saying nothing.

Now all the tribesmen knew that to see a ghost or a spirit of the jungle was nearly always a sign of approaching death.

'Go away!' screamed the hunter to Timakana. 'Go away or I will shoot you.'

Seizing his bow, the hunter shot arrow after arrow into the bushes towards Timakana, but his hands were shaking so much that he missed every time. In desperation he snatched up a burning log from the fire and rushed at the staring creature.

At last the hunter seemed to be making some impression on his tormentor. The spirit turned and limped away into the forest. The hunter chased after it, brandishing the burning wood. Satisfied that he had driven Timakana away, the hunter returned

to his fire, only to find Timakana sitting there waiting.

'What can I do?' moaned the unfortunate tortoise hunter. 'What is this creature that has such power?'

The jungle spirit rose to his feet and clashed his swollen knees together. The rattling of the calabashes sent the horrible sound 'te-wo-yi' echoing around the forest.

Cold with fear, the hunter took a branch from the palm tree. He held it in the fire until it blazed with a dozen tongues of flame. He rushed at Timakana and this time drove him far away into the forest. The limping figure swayed and rattled out of sight.

Sighing with relief and thinking he had driven the spirit away at last, the hunter returned to his fireside. There was Timakana sitting waiting for him, smiling a thin, joyless smile and staring with unblinking, red eyes.

The hunter did not dare to sit by his fire. Least of all did he try to go to sleep. Instead he stood among the bushes until dawn. As the sun rose, Timakana stood up and walked a few paces from the fireside. He looked at the hunter and smiled his thin smile again and then he went away.

The sun rose above the horizon. The hunter took up his bow and his hammock and stumbled back to his home.

'What is the matter with you?' asked his wife.

'Timakana was with me all night and he has eaten my soul,' said the hunter. He fell down and lay for five days without eating or drinking. Then he died.

As every tribesman knows, the hunter need not have died. But he did two very foolish things. He spoke rudely to Timakana, who is the friend of Curupir and very powerful. Anyone who meets Timakana should speak to him politely, then he will do no harm. However, the hunter's second mistake was even worse. He told his wife that he had seen a spirit. Anyone who sees a spirit and talks about it, will die for sure. Spirits are secret creatures and do not like to be gossiped about.

13

The Great Flood

Every tribesman from the south to the north of South America knows that, long ago, there was a great flood. Before the flood, some people lived in fine stone cities linked by good roads. The roads were guarded and safe. People had to pay to travel along them, but they knew they would not be robbed during their journey.

Other people lived like savages on the plains, hunting and gathering vegetables. They were homeless.

One day an old man married a beautiful young wife. The wife was discontented. She stood on the banks of a great river. 'Overflow! Overflow!' she begged the river. 'Cover the whole land.'

So the river overflowed and many people were drowned, but the beautiful young wife fled into the sky to live with the moon.

Away in the valley a peasant was tethering his llama to graze, but the llama was restless and kept tugging at the rope.

'What is the matter with you?' asked the peasant. 'Why will you not let me tether you?'

'I do not wish to be tethered here,' replied the llama. 'Soon a great flood will come and we shall be drowned.'

The peasant was naturally greatly alarmed and asked the llama what he should do.

'Collect food for five days. Take your family and me to the top of a high mountain,' replied the llama.

The peasant, his family and the llama went up into the mountains. They saw the waters of the river flood the plain. They saw the waves of the sea rise up and wash over the land. For five days the floods rose, until they were lapping round the peasants and the llama as they stood on the highest mountain range. All the animals were driven up to the mountains with them.

Gradually the waters went down, the sea rolled back from the land, and the river lay once more in its bed. Almost everyone on earth had been drowned by this flood. Then the man and his family and the llama came down from the mountains. All the people now living are descended from that family.

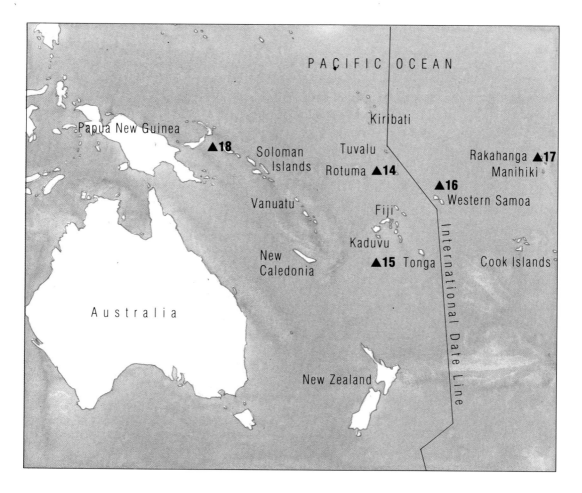

The Pacific

14

The Giant with Teeth of Fire

The Fiji Islands lie in the Pacific Ocean, north of the tip of New Zealand and east of the Great Barrier Reef. The Samoan and Tongan Islands are to the north-east, while the Solomon and New Hebrides Islands lie in a north-south chain to the west. There are considerable distances between the islands, but similar folk tales and legends, obviously from a common origin, are found all over the Pacific.

Long ago, a giant lived in a cave high up on the side of one of the mountains of the island of Rotuma, to the north of the Fiji Islands. He was not an ordinary giant because his teeth burned like coals of fire. Every time he opened his mouth, heat like a furnace blasted out before him. If he drew back his huge lips in one of his frightful smiles, the glare from his burning teeth outshone the sun.

Fortunately, the giant slept in his cave most of the time, but sometimes he would rouse himself and stride down the mountain. He would open his mouth and breathe out streams of heat and flame. He would grin in all directions and singe the leaves of the trees with the glare of his blazing teeth.

The villagers who lived on the lower slopes of the mountains by the sea, ran away whenever they saw the giant approaching. They dreaded his coming. They prayed that he would sleep forever in his cave.

Some of the brave young men looked with longing at the fire that streamed from the giant's teeth. In those days the people of Rotuma did not know how to make fire.

'If only we could steal a little fire from the giant, how much better life would be,' thought the young men. 'Our women could cook delicious meals. We could have warmth and light in the chill of the dark nights.'

So the bravest and most daring of the young men of Rotuma

got together. They took bundles of dried coconut palm leaves and crept cautiously up the side of the mountain towards the giant's cave. Outside the cave they stood and listened. There was no sound. Feeling very brave, they crept into the cave.

The giant lay sound asleep, breathing deeply. With every outward breath, his huge, thick lips parted, letting out a glow of light from his burning teeth. With every puff of breath, tongues of flame bubbled out into the cave, only to be sucked back into that enormous mouth.

The brave young men crept forward, using the light from the giant's teeth to see the stones on the cave floor. They did not want to stumble or make a noise.

Closer and closer they crept. At last the young men were able to hold out the bundles of dried leaves so that the little flames dancing round the giant's mouth reached them and set them alight. Then the young men turned and ran away down the mountain side.

But they did not escape so easily. In his excitement, one of the young men had let his hand quiver. The leaves had tickled the lips of the giant, who stirred and then woke. Blinking his eyes, he caught sight of the light from the burning leaves, flickering away down the mountain side.

The giant rose to his feet in a rage. 'Who dares to steal my fire?' he roared. Long flames darted from his burning teeth. 'No one on this island but ME may have fire!'

He shook himself and, rubbing the sleep from his eyes, stamped down the mountain side after the brave young men.

Luckily the young men were swift. Holding the precious burning coconut leaves, they ran into the cave where they lived and rolled a huge boulder across the entrance. Then the young men lit a wood fire from the burning leaves. At last they could eat cooked food and keep warm.

Meanwhile, the giant stood outside the cave. He pushed at the rock. He stamped. He shouted. The rock did not move. The giant breathed fire over the rock, but it stayed in one piece.

Then the giant had an idea. He bent close to the rock and called in a sweet voice, 'Let us be friends. Push the rock aside so that I may sing to you.'

The young men did not believe that the giant wanted to be friends, but they also did not wish to stay in their cave forever.

'Let us give him part of what he wants and perhaps he will go away,' they said.

The brave young men moved the rock, making a small gap at the entrance to their cave. At once the giant tried to push in his head, but it did not fit.

'That is not wide enough,' he said. 'You will never hear my lovely song through that narrow hole. Push the boulder further aside.'

By this time the brave young men had thought of a plan.

'Very well,' they called. They pushed the rock to one side so that the giant could easily thrust his head into the cave.

The giant drew in a deep breath and thrust his head forward, ready to open his mouth and breath out flames and heat from his burning teeth.

Soon there will be nothing but cinders left of these impudent young men, he thought.

But he was wrong.

The moment the giant's head was through the gap, the young men rolled the rock forward, crushing the giant's head flat. The giant was dead. His flaming teeth spluttered and grew cold and dark. The young men ran from the cave shouting and calling the people from all the villages around.

'We have killed the giant!' they laughed. 'His teeth no longer burn with fire, but the fire is not lost. We have it. Now life will be pleasant for us all.'

The brave and generous young men shared the flames with everyone on the island. Soon a fire blazed in every hut and the lovely smell of cooking yams and fish filled the air. And best of all, the islanders no longer lived in fear of the giant with teeth of fire.

15

The Great Shark God

This is another story from the Fiji Islands. Kadavu Island lies in the south-west section of the main Fiji Islands group.

The swelling waves of the Pacific Ocean heaved and rolled from island to island. Everything that was important in the world seemed to be above the surface of the bright blue Fijian sea. But beneath the waves, there lay another world ruled by the sharks.

The great god of the sharks was called Dakuwaqa. He was big and quarrelsome, a brawling fighter. He was always looking for trouble and usually he found it.

In those days, when the world was young, each island had its own guardian. The guardian was usually a shark, which lived beside the reef at the entrance to the island. Only friends and those willing to pay tribute to the guardian were allowed to enter.

Dakuwaqa liked to think he was the greatest of the guardians. He often fought with other guardian sharks and he always won. Usually the struggle was so fierce that their thrashing bodies sent tidal waves washing over the beaches and up the rivers of the islands, drowning many people and flooding their homes.

Dakuwaqa did not care. All he thought of was fighting, and winning, and making all the other guardian sharks pay tribute to him. He was the great god of the sharks and that was the way things were going to stay.

One day Dakuwaqa was swimming towards Beqa in the Fiji Islands, when he met an old friend called Masilaca. Masilaca was also a shark god, although not as powerful as Dakuwaqa, but he was a mischief maker.

'I hear you have recently won a great fight at Lomaiviti,' Masilaca greeted his friend.

'I did indeed,' he agreed. 'A fine monster was living there. He thought he could challenge me. ME! What stupidity! He will be making no more challenges, I can tell you!'

'I am sure he will not,' smiled Masilaca. 'You are a wonderful fighter, Dakuwaqa.'

After a pause, he added, 'I notice you never swim to Kadavu Island. Of course, it cannot be that you are frightened, not YOU! Perhaps you are just being cautious. After all, you have always won all your fights. Why go to an island where you might lose? Why risk your reputation? You are quite right to visit only islands where you are sure of finding guardians whom you can beat. You are as wise as you are courageous, Dakuwaqa!'

Dakuwaqa lashed his tail in fury. 'How dare you say that I am afraid to swim to Kadavu Island!' he bellowed. 'I have not been there because I thought it was not worth visiting. What is there at Kadavu Island?'

Masilaca circled round, well out of the reach of Dakuwaqa. 'They say that a mighty monster guards the land so that no one dares to go ashore,' he called. 'And they also say that the guardian of the reef is a creature such as has never been seen before. No one knows how to fight it. Everyone is frightened. People are whispering that you are frightened as well. I said that you were frightened of nothing, but then people ask, "Well, why doesn't he swim to Kadavu Island then?"'

Long before Masilaca had finished speaking, Dakuwaqa started beating his huge tail from side to side and slid through the sea towards Kadavu. He could not bear to think that any creature in the sea could be mightier than himself.

As Dakuwaqa neared the island, he heard a low throbbing voice calling to him from the shore. For the first time in his life, Dakuwaqa felt a cold shiver of fear run down his back.

He swam on. The voice was strange and disturbing, but it came from the land. Nothing on the land could hurt Dakuwaqa, a god of the sea.

The voice called again, 'I am Tui Vesi, the guardian of the vesi tree. I know you have come to challenge the power of the gods of this island. How I long to fight you, but I cannot leave the land and you cannot rise out of the sea. Go, my friend. Swim to the gap in the reef and there you will find a monster, such as you have never met before. He will fight on my behalf. He will teach you not to come to Kadavu Island with your eyes bright with insolence.'

By this time, Dakuwaqa was in a fury. He roared through the water towards the razor-sharp gap in the reef where the ocean boiled in and out. His eyes darted to and fro, looking for the guardian shark. But he saw nothing.

Dakuwaqa swam on. Suddenly an arm lashed out from a cave and wrapped itself round his body. He gasped and struggled. Then another arm curled round his tail, stopping Dakuwaqa from moving. A third arm twined round the shark god's head, holding his jaws together so that he could not bite a thing. The guardian of Kadavu Island was a giant octopus and it held Dakuwaqa helpless in its grip.

Dakuwaqa had met his match at last. The arms of the mighty octopus squeezed tighter and tighter until the strength left Dakuwaqa's body. He was about to die.

Although his teeth were clenched together by the pressure of the octopus's arms, Dakuwaqa managed to squeeze out a few words. For the first time in his bullying life, he begged for mercy.

'Will you pay tribute to me?' asked the octopus.

'Yes!' gasped Dakuwaqa.

'Will you pay tribute to my master Tui Vesi, the guardian of the vesi tree?'

'Yes!!' groaned Dakuwaqa.

'Will you promise never to attack the fishermen of Kadavu Island and to guard them wherever they go?' asked the octopus with an extra squeeze.

'YES!!!' moaned Dakuwaqa, quite sure that his last moment had come.

'Then you may go free,' said the octopus. He released the god of the sharks, who rolled weakly to the sand of the ocean bed.

When Dakuwaqa had regained his strength, he swam the waters of the Pacific again. The other sharks were still afraid of him, but Dakuwaqa kept his promise to the guardian of Kadavu.

To this day, while the men of other islands fear the sharks, the men of Kadavu ride happily in their canoes. They know that Dakuwaqa is protecting them and that no other shark will dare to attack.

16

The Giant Turtle

This story comes from the Fiji Islands in the middle of the vast Pacific Ocean. It was told by the Fijians to explain how it was that there were people from the islands of Tonga living among them.

There was once a fisherman from Samoa, named Lekabai, who was carried far out to sea by a sudden storm. The wind blew relentlessly and the waves raced ever onward. The spray blinded Lekabai's eyes and swamped his boat. Finally, the unfortunate man felt the familiar boards of his canoe sink away from under him, and he was left struggling in the vast sea. Suddenly his waving hands brushed against a solid rock. He pulled himself on to a ledge and climbed out of reach of the stinging spray.

As he rested, Lekabai soon found that, although he had been saved from drowning, he was by no means safe. He was on a narrow, barren rock that stretched up towards the clouds. Lekabai hoped that if he climbed high enough, he might find water and food, or even people. He began clambering up the steep rock face. He drank rainwater from crevices, but found no food.

Lekabai climbed to the clouds, and through them, but still the rock stretched upwards. After several days, he collapsed. When he opened his eyes he found himself lying on soft turf in a land of gentle breezes where food grew and birds sang.

Lekabai was able to eat and regain his strength, but even so he was not happy. Lekabai missed his home and family in Samoa, so he sat and wept.

Now the land into which Lekabai had climbed was the realm of the Sky King. No weeping was ever heard in that perfect place, so the Sky King hurried to Lekabai and asked him what was wrong.

Lekabai realised that he was talking to a god. He spoke with respect and explained that although this kingdom was perfect, he, a humble Samoan, could not help feeling homesick.

The Sky King smiled on Lekabai and said, 'Weep no more. I will lend you a sacred turtle on which you may ride back to your home. Sit on the back of the turtle and cover your eyes. Whatever happens, do not look at anything until you feel the turtle crawl up the beach of your island in Samoa. If you open your eyes on the journey, that will be the end of you.'

Lekabai thanked the Sky King. He was climbing on to the back of the huge turtle when the Sky King added, 'If you wish to thank me, give the turtle a coconut and a mat woven of coconut leaves to bring back to me here in the sky. We have no coconuts and I have heard that they are delicious. Send me one and we will grow trees. Send me a mat and we will learn to weave our own by copying yours.'

Lekabai agreed willingly. He shut his eyes and covered them with his hands. He sat on the back of the turtle as it crawled towards the edge of the rocky pinnacle on which they all stood.

The turtle leaped from the rock and fell through the air like a stone. Lekabai was terrified, but he kept his hands over his eyes, gripping the shell of the turtle with his legs. They hit the sea with a mighty crash and plunged deep beneath its surface.

The sharks swam around them and brushed against Lekabai with their rough skins. 'Open your eyes,' they hissed. 'These are dangerous waters. Surely you should look where you are going!'

Although he was shaking with fright, Lekabai remembered the words of the Sky King and kept his hands firmly over his eyes.

Up, up through the water they rose until they broke into the air and the light. Now dolphins plunged through the waves at their side. 'What a foolish man to cover his eyes!' they laughed. 'Open your eyes and look where you are going.'

Still Lekabai kept his hands over his eyes and clung to the back of the turtle with his legs.

As the strange pair neared Samoa, the sea birds flocked around them. 'Here is Lekabai returned from the dead!' they screeched. 'Open your eyes, Lekabai. Look where you are going or the sea will take you away again.'

Still Lekabai remembered the words of the Sky King and did not open his eyes. He waited until the turtle had waddled on to the hot sand. Only then did Lekabai take his hands from his eyes. He looked round and saw his home and his wife and his children and he was happy.

Everyone on the island was amazed at Lekabai's return. They

thought that he had been drowned weeks ago. A great feast was made and there was laughing and dancing for the rest of the day.

Suddenly Lekabai remembered his promise to give a coconut and a mat of coconut leaves to the turtle. He hurried back to the beach, but the turtle was nowhere to be seen. It had grown tired of waiting and had swum out to the reef to eat seaweed.

Lekabai hurried to a canoe and was paddling towards the turtle, when he saw a boat full of returning fishermen stop by the reef. They speared the turtle, thinking that they had made a fine catch to complete a good day at sea.

How Lekabai wailed and wept. 'The Sky King will never forgive me!' he groaned. 'We shall all be punished for this terrible deed.'

Everyone on the island was frightened. They decided to bury the body of the turtle so deep that the Sky King would never know what had happened.

All the men of the island joined together and dug for five days. They put a tall palm tree into the hole so that they could climb up and down its stem with the loads of earth. On the sixth day they put the turtle in the hole together with a coconut and a mat woven of coconut leaves. Then they covered everything over and hoped that all would be forgotten.

The Sky King did know what had happened, but for some reason his anger was not great. He did not punish Lekabai or the people of the island. Instead he sent a bird to hover over the grave of the turtle. As the last of the earth was being thrown into the hole, the bird swooped down and gently touched a boy called Lavai-pani. Nothing more happened.

The years went by and all seemed well. Lekabai grew old and died. His children grew old and died, and their children grew old and died. The strange thing was that the boy, Lavai-pani, never grew old. He never grew up. He stayed a fresh-faced child for year after year after year.

Many more years passed. One day the King of the Islands of Tonga heard the legend of the great turtle that was buried deep on an island of Samoa.

'I should like the shell of that turtle. It would make many fish hooks,' he said. He looked at a group of his young men. 'Go to Samoa and fetch that turtle shell,' he ordered.

The young men sailed in a large canoe to Samoa, but when they arrived and explained their mission, everyone laughed.

'We all know that old legend,' smiled the Samoans, 'but it is only a legend. No one knows where the turtle was buried, or if there was a turtle at all!'

The young men sailed back to Tonga and told their King that the shell of the great turtle could not be found.

The King flew into a terrible rage. 'Go back to Samoa,' he shouted, 'and return here with the shell of the great turtle. If you come back empty-handed for a second time, I will kill you.'

The young men fell over each other in their haste to set sail. They reached Samoa and spoke to the oldest men in the villages.

'Surely you remember where the great turtle was buried?' they asked.

The grey-haired old men shook their heads and laughed. 'We cannot help you. It is an old story, nothing more.'

Then a strange young boy, who had been young for as long as memory lasted, stepped forward. It was Lavai-pani, the boy who had been touched by the bird sent by the Sky King.

'Do not be distressed, men of Tonga,' he said. 'I will show you where the great turtle was buried. I was there when it was done.'

He walked to a spot along the beach and pointed.

'The turtle was buried there,' he said.

The Tongans could scarcely believe Lavai-pani's story. How could a boy so young have been present at the burial of the turtle? However, his was the only help they had, so they started to dig. They dug all day and found nothing. All the while the Samoan villagers stood at the edge of the hole looking down at the Tongans and laughing.

'Fancy believing that crazy boy,' they jeered. 'You will never find anything.'

The Tongans dug for another day and still they found nothing. They spoke angrily to Lavai-pani. They said their very lives depended on finding the turtle shell and, if they had to sail home without the shell and so to their deaths, they would take Lavai-pani to die with them.

Then it was the turn of Lavai-pani to laugh and the Samoans stared at the boy, for they had never heard him laugh before.

'These Tongans have already sailed twice to and from Tonga, and yet they complain at a little digging,' chuckled Lavai-pani. 'Listen to me. Dig for three more days and you will find the shell of the sacred turtle. Or give up and go home. I don't care.'

In desperation the Tongans carried on with their digging. On the evening of the fifth day, they found the body of the turtle but, strange to say, neither the coconut nor the mat was there.

Perhaps they had found their way to the Sky King after all.

Filled with joy, the Tongans loaded the turtle shell into their canoe and hurried home. On the way they decided that, after all their exertions, they deserved to keep some of the turtle shell for themselves. When they arrived in Tonga, they gave twelve pieces of turtle shell to the King and left the thirteenth piece hidden in their canoe.

The King could not be deceived so easily. 'All the shell is not here,' he raged. 'Where is the thirteenth piece?'

None of the young men dared to tell the furious king that they had kept back a piece of shell. Instead, one of them spoke up and said that it had been kept by the people of Samoa.

'In that case,' roared the King, 'go back and get it. I tell you, I am to be feared more than the people of Samoa.'

The unfortunate young men climbed into their canoe and sailed out into the vast ocean. They did not want to go back to Samoa again and they were afraid and tired of their bullying King, so they let the wind blow them where it would.

After many weeks they came at last to Kadavu, one of the Fiji Islands, which was then ruled by King Rewa. He was kind to the weary young men and gave them land on which to live. They built houses and took wives and were happy. So it came about that the first people from Tonga settled in the islands of Fiji.

17

The Voyages of Shame

Long ago, a skilled sailor named Here lived on the island of Manihiki in the Cook Islands. Here was married to Muhu, a lovely woman who had several brothers.

It was the custom of the Manihiki people to live on their island while the food lasted. Then, when the crops were all eaten, they would climb into their boats and sail across the Pacific Ocean to the island of Rakahanga, to eat the food which was growing there. When the food on Rakahanga was eaten, they would return to Manihiki. Before they left either Rakahanga or Manihiki, the people would plant food to grow during their absence. So it had been for as long as anyone could remember.

The journey from Manihiki to Rakahanga was hazardous, and the canoes had to be carefully prepared before setting sail. Single canoes were lashed together to make big double ones and the sails were made from handwoven mats, strong and new.

Official canoes sailed ahead of the main fleet carrying the most important families and the wise men. Piloted by the most skilled sailors, the official party led the way over the long, rolling waves. They landed first on Rakahanga to inspect the sacred grounds and do everything that must be done to make the great gods happy. Then the wise men would declare Rakahanga safe and allow the rest of the people to land.

In spite of all these precautions, some canoes were always lost on the voyage. The vast sea was a dangerous place.

Here was a proud and ambitious man. He smiled at the important people and pushed himself forward until he was included in the official party which sailed first from Manihiki to Rakahanga.

Here deserved to be among the important people. He was a fine sailor. He could stand in a swaying canoe and feel the long, regular swell that always came from the same direction. Sometimes he stood with his eyes closed and felt a change in the rhythm of movement. This meant that the canoe was down-sea

from an island that had broken the movement of the swell.

He knew that birds flew out from islands to feed in the daytime and flew out from the islands to feed in daytime and flew back to roost in the evening. He also knew that, as evening fell, a canoe which followed the flight of the birds would find an island on which to land.

Here was a useful man and deserved to travel with the important official party, but he would not take his wife with him in this special group.

'You have many brothers,' he said to his wife. 'Travel with them in their canoes.' He did not want his wife bothering him while he was talking with important people.

So Muhu stayed behind and travelled with her brothers on the first voyage after their marriage. Here landed first on Rakahanga and visited the sacred grounds with the wise men, and took part in all the grand ceremonies. When they were over, he went to the beach and waited for Muhu to arrive.

'Come along. Come along,' he called, as she scrambled ashore. 'Go to our house. There is work to be done.'

Muhu went with her husband, but she felt ashamed that she had been left behind with her brothers, like a woman without a husband.

The same thing happened on the return journey. Here did not ask his wife to accompany him in the official canoes, as he could not be bothered with her. She travelled in shame with her brothers, a neglected wife.

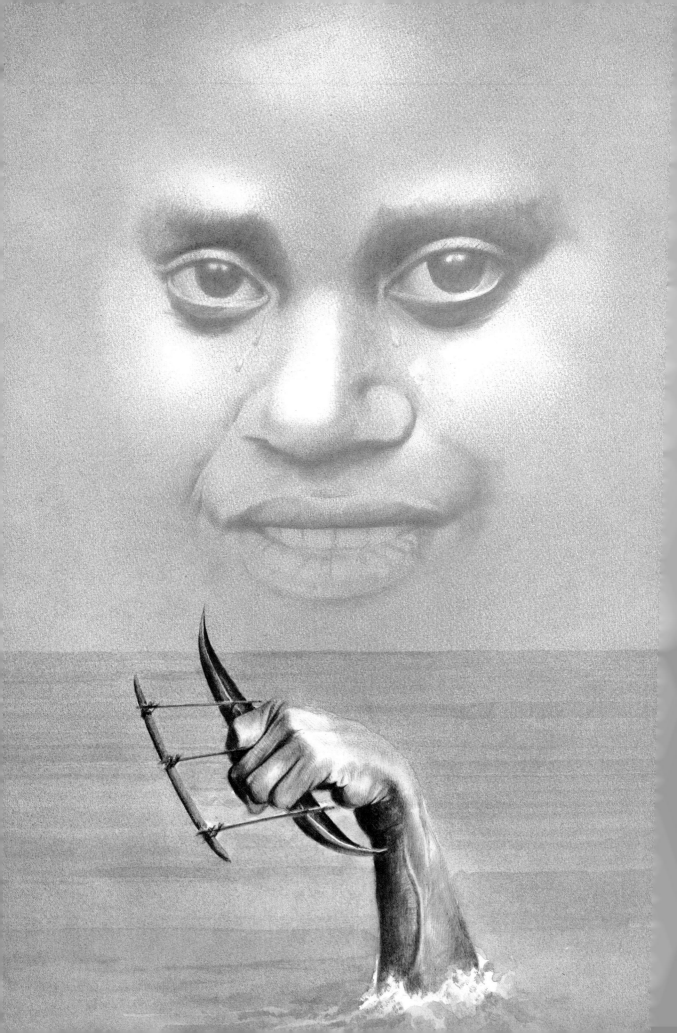

For several seasons Muhu tried her best to please her unkind husband, hoping that he would ask to have her included in the official party. But he did not.

As one voyage from Rakahanga to Manihiki was almost completed and they were within sight of shore, Muhu said to her brothers, 'Untie my canoe from yours. You can paddle safely to the island in a single canoe from this short distance. I would like to travel further on my own.'

Her brothers knew that Muhu could bear the shame no longer. She intended to paddle out into the vast ocean and end her life. Once a small canoe was caught by an ocean current, no one could ever paddle back to the island.

The brothers tried to dissuade their sister from doing this, but Muhu had put up with Here's neglect for too long. She was certain that he would never treat her with respect.

So the brothers unlashed the canoe. They reached Manihiki, but Muhu was carried on by the long, swelling waves.

Here was waiting out on the reef.

'Where is Muhu?' he asked in surprise, at the sight of the single canoe.

The brothers were so distressed with grief and so angry at Here, that they could not reply. They turned their faces away and paddled to shore.

'Where is Muhu?' shouted Here, scrambling along the reef.

At last one of the brothers called, 'Turn your eyes to where the sea meets the sky. There you will see Muhu.'

Here looked out to sea and saw the lone canoe drifting swiftly away on the strong current. He flung himself into the sea and tried to swim after his wife, to bring her back to the island. He did not succeed.

Hours later, he struggled exhausted on to the reef. The other islanders stared at him in silence. Everyone blamed him for the death of a good woman.

Here wailed and moaned. He slashed his skin with coral to show his regret. Still no one spoke to him. He had treated his wife very badly and this disaster had been his own fault. So Here lived alone for the rest of his life because no other woman would ever marry him.

18

How Coconuts Came to New Guinea

All over the islands of New Guinea, stories are told about how the coconut tree first grew from a human head. Whose head it was and why it was buried in strange circumstances varies with each tale, but the linking of the growth of a coconut tree with a buried body, usually on the beach, remains the same.

Long ago, so people say, there were no coconuts on the island of Salimum. People ate taros and yams and bananas and tapioca, and they caught fish, but they ate no coconuts.

There was one man who was an expert fisherman, but he did not like gardening. He fished from dawn until dusk and caught fine hauls, but he would not bend his back to plant and hoe and weed. This man hawked his fish from hut to hut, asking the other islanders to exchange vegetables and fruit for his fish. At first they gave the fisherman some of their yams or bananas or a portion of tapioca, but eventually they grew impatient with his requests.

'We can catch all the fish we want for ourselves,' they said. 'Fish are plentiful. We work hard to grow food in our gardens; why should we give it to this lazy man? We do not need his fish. If he cannot bother to tend a garden, let him eat only fish. If he grows bored with fish, that is his problem, not ours.'

All the islanders agreed that they would refuse to exchange any more fruit and vegetables for fish.

On the evening of the next day, the fisherman returned at sunset. He came back much later than the other men because he had fished for many hours in order to catch enough fish to exchange for other food. He was tired and burned by the sun that had shone mercilessly down on the little fishing boats.

Wearily the man went to a hut where a fire was lit and the delicious smell of cooking food filled the air. To his amazement he was ordered away, his fish were rejected and he was given no tasty vegetables. He went to the next hut and the next, but everywhere his treatment was the same. No one would take his fish and no one would give him vegetables or fruit.

If the man had been wise, he would have gone home to rest. But he was sick of fish, which he had been handling all day, and was longing for the taste of vegetables. So he lit a bamboo stick and went in search of wild yams. They were not as plump as the garden yams, but they were better than nothing.

He walked through the darkness away from the village and at last he found the food he sought. He blew on the stick to make a better light, then he tied the bamboo torch to his back and with his hands free, bent over to dig.

The fisherman was so tired and hungry that he did not notice when the fire caught his hair and the flames spread to his clothes. He fell forward into the hole he was digging and there he died. The next day the islanders found his body. They covered it over where it lay because the man had no relatives who wished to mourn his death. Within a month the man was forgotten. He had been a nuisance and, in their hearts, the islanders were glad to be rid of him.

To everyone's surprise, a strange plant started to grow up out of the fisherman's grave.

'Perhaps the plant is magical. Perhaps it is sent by the spirits,' said the islanders.

They watered and tended the strange plant. It grew tall and developed a thick trunk. After a

while it bore green fruit that turned brown and fell to the ground. When the islanders cut the fruit open, they found that it had a mouth and eyes, like a human face. Then they were sure that it had grown from the head of the strange fisherman. That fruit was a coconut.

On a nearby island, a very different story was told. A beautiful maiden, named Ina, loved to swim in a clear rock pool near her home. One day, as the lovely Ina was bathing in the pool, she felt something brush against her leg. It was an enormous eel. The girl was terrified and scrambled out of the water. Turning to look back into the depths, she saw the eel curled up at the bottom of the pool.

The next day, when Ina went to the pool, there was no sign of the eel. As the day was hot, the girl slid into the cool water. At once she saw the huge eel circling her as she swam. It looked at her with big gentle eyes and suddenly all her fear left her.

Ina continued to swim and the eel did her no harm as they played together in the pool. For weeks the two unusual companions swam and circled together in the water.

One day, when Ina was sitting on the rocks drying her hair, the eel climbed out beside her and, to the girl's amazement, it turned into a tall young man.

'I am Tuna, the god of the eels,' he said. 'It is my duty to swim in the streams and protect the eels, but when I saw how beautiful you were as you swam in the pool, I could think only of you.'

Tuna and Ina were married and lived happily together. While Tuna was with Ina, he had the appearance of a handsome young man. When she left him to work in her garden or visit her friends,

he resumed the shape of an eel and swam in the pools and streams.

One day Tuna slithered from the pool and stood in his human form before Ina. 'The gods are angry with me,' he said. 'They say I am neglecting my duty and I may not stay with you. A flood is being sent as a punishment and there is only one way I can save you. Promise me that you will do exactly as I tell you.'

Ina was heartbroken that she was to be parted from her beloved. However she had little choice but to obey him.

'The flood will surround your home,' said Tuna. 'The water will lap at your door, then an eel will swim up from the water and lay its head on your doorstep. You must cut off its head and bury the head near your house. You will be saved and you will also receive a parting gift of great value from me.'

Tearfully Ina agreed, without realising what she had agreed to do. Tuna said goodbye and swam away through the shifting waters. Rain fell heavily all through the night and floods ran down from the hills. The next day Ina's house was surrounded by rising waters and she feared for her life, until she saw a rippling near her door. An eel laid its head on the doorstep.

With a quick blow from an axe, Ina severed the head. It turned immediately into Tuna's head. Ina screamed with horror, but still she was brave enough to do as her dear husband had asked. Already the flood waters were receding, so the weeping girl buried the head near her hut.

A few weeks later, to her surprise, a strange plant grew from the very spot where she had buried the head. Wondering if this might be the gift of which Tuna had spoken, Ina tended the new growth with all her love. The shoot grew into a tree. The tree sprouted leaves, then it bore fruit that ripened and fell to the ground.

When Ina broke away the brown husk, she saw two eyes and a mouth looking at her from the fruit beneath. It seemed as if Tuna was staring at her. Ina knew that this new fruit, which she called the coconut, was the gift that Tuna had promised her. The food from the coconut has been a blessing to the islands ever since.